Animals at School

by Michèle Dufresne

Contents

PIONEER VALLEY EDUCATIONAL PRESS, INC.

CHAPTER 1
A Pig at School

One day, a pig
got out of his pen.
He walked down the street
and into the school playground.

"Look," shouted the children.
"There's a pig!
Look at the pig!"

The children ran to tell
the principal about the pig.
"He's big and black,"
they told the principal.

"A *pig*?" said the principal.
"A pig on the playground?"

"Oh dear! Oh dear!"
said the principal.
"The children are not
doing their work.
They're all looking at the pig!
We can't have a pig
at our school."

"We like having a pig
at school,"
said the preschoolers.

"Let's write a song about the pig," said the teacher.

One Black Pig
One black pig

The preschoolers wrote a song about the pig.
Then they made pig noses and sang their song.

The kindergartners also wrote
about the pig who came to school.
Then they put their story
in the hall
for everyone to read.

The first graders
wrote stories, too.
They made their stories
into books, and then everyone
read their stories.
"Well," said the principal.
"Maybe it was OK for the pig
to come to school."

CHAPTER 2
Thistle is Lost

In Room 5, there is a rabbit named Thistle.

The children take care
of Thistle.
They feed Thistle
carrots and apples,
and they help the teacher
clean Thistle's cage.

Sometimes they leave
the cage door open
and Thistle runs around
the classroom.

One day, someone left
the classroom door open.
"Oh no," said the teacher.
"Where is Thistle?"

"Oh no," said the children.
"The classroom door is open.
Thistle has run away!"

"Go to the office
and tell the principal
that Thistle is missing,"
said the teacher.

"Thistle has run away,"
the children told the principal.

"Oh no!" said the principal.

"First we had a pig
on the playground.
Now there is a rabbit
running around
somewhere in the school!"

"Hmmm, how can we get
Thistle back?"
asked the principal.

"Thistle loves apples.
Let's put an apple
in the hall,"
said the children.

The children and the principal
put an apple in the hall.
Soon, Thistle came out
to eat the apple.
"Good," said the principal.
"Now go and write a story
about how you found Thistle!"